T2-BQD-289
D0538356

For J, F, M, A, M, J, J, A, S, O, N, and D—year after year after year

BEACH LANE BOOKS • An imprint of Simon & Schuster Children's Publishing Division • 1230 Avenue of the Americas, New York, New York 10020 • Copyright © 2016 by Keith Baker • All rights reserved, including the right of reproduction in whole or in part in any form. • BEACH LANE BOOKS is a trademark of Simon & Schuster, Inc. • For information about special discounts for bulk purchases, please contact Simon & Schuster Special Sales at 1-866-506-1949 or business@simonandschuster.com. • The Simon & Schuster Speakers Bureau can bring authors to your live event. For more information or to book an event, contact the Simon & Schuster Speakers Bureau at 1-866-248-3049 or visit our website at www.simonspeakers.com. • Book design by Sonia Chaghatzbanian • The text for this book is set in Frankfurter Medium. • The illustrations for this book are rendered digitally. • Manufactured in China • 0816 SCP • First Edition • Library of Congress Cataloging-in-Publication Data • Baker, Keith, 1953- author. • Hap-pea all year / Keith Baker.—First edition. • p. cm. • Summary: In rhyming text, a group of happy green peas celebrates the special holidays of each month, and the passing seasons. • ISBN 978-1-4814-5854-2 (hardcover : alk. paper) • ISBN 978-1-4814-5855-9 (eBook) • 1. Peas—Juvenile fiction. 2. Seasons—Juvenile fiction. 3. Holidays—Juvenile fiction. 4. Stories in rhyme. [1. Stories in rhyme. 2. Peas—Fiction. 3. Seasons—Fiction. 4. Holidays—Fiction.] I. Title. • PZ8.3.B175Hap 2015 • 813.54—dc23 • [E] • 2015020891 • 10 9 8 7 6 5 4 3 2 1

aker, Keith, 1953-
ap-pea all year! /
2016]
3305237370857
a 12/20/16

Keith Baker

Hap-pea all YEAR

Beach Lane Books New York London Toronto Sydney New Delhi

Hap-pea January! Let's get going.

Grab your mittens—*hooray, it's snowing!*

Hap-pea February! Deliver valentines.

Count to twenty-eight—or leap to twenty-nine.

Hap-pea March! Wear a touch of green,

and look for leprechauns on day seventeen.

Hap-pea April! Walk through squishy mud.

Splash in every puddle—*behold!* A flower bud.

Hap-pea May! Grease up the rusty bike. Two flat tires—

who wants to take a hike?

Hap-pea June! Pack up—school's over!

Clean out your messy desk, roll in summer clover.

Hap-pea July! Chase the fireflies.

Roll out a sleeping bag, watch the sparkling skies.

Hap-pea August! Bait a fishing hook.

Nap in cool shade, reread your favorite book.

Hap-pea September! Grab paper and a pen.

Greet your eager teachers—school begins again.

Hap-pea October! Carve a toothy smile.

Rake up all the leaves, jump in every pile.

Hap-pea November! Open the sidewalk gate.

Welcome all your guests, fill every empty plate.

Hap-pea December! Tie a shiny bow.

Light a glowing candle, drink some hot cocoa.

Now gather all around—pull each other near.

Together we will have another . . .

January
February
May
June
August
October

hap-pea . . .

hap-pea . . .

P
mine

SCHOOL

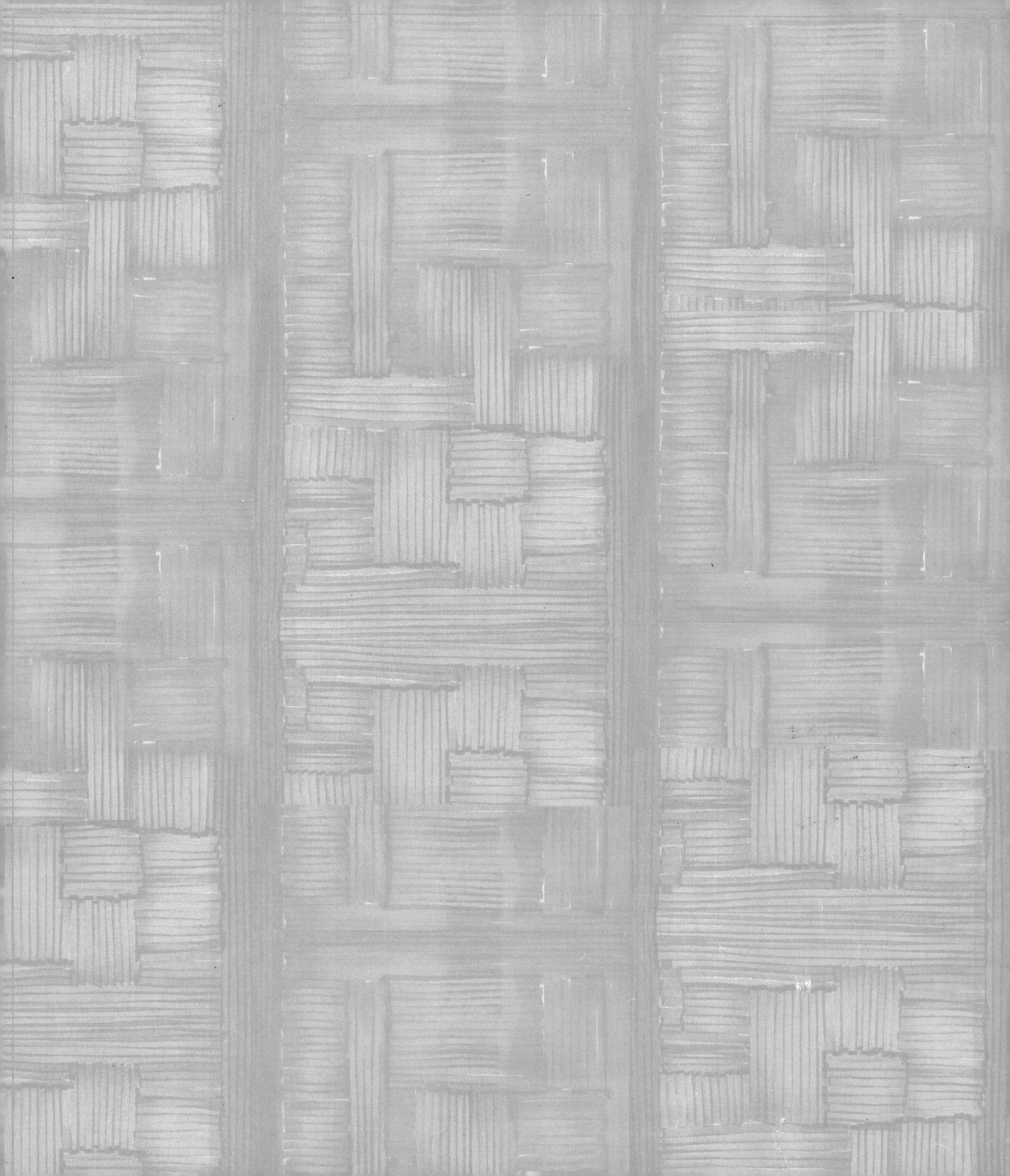